The Wonky Donkey

A Red Fox Book

Published by Random House Children's Books
20 Vauxhall Bridge Road, London SW1V 2SA

A division of The Random House Group Ltd
London Melbourne Sydney Auckland
Johannesburg and agencies throughout the world

1 3 5 7 9 10 8 6 4 2

First published in Great Britain by
The Bodley Head Children's Books 1999
Red Fox edition 2000

Printed in Singapore by Tien Wah Press (PTE) Ltd

The RANDOM HOUSE Group Limited Reg. No. 954009

ISBN 0 09 926396 3
www.randomhouse.co.uk

Visit Korky Paul's website on:
www.korkypaul.com

For Dad, and all people with multiple sclerosis - J.L.

The Wonky Donkey

Jonathan Long and Korky Paul

RED FOX

There once was a donkey all tatty and grey. For ten long years he had worked himself to the bone for a cruel owner.

No matter how many heavy pots and stones and logs he carried, not once did the owner thank him.

Never mind thanks – he hardly even fed him. And at night he gave him a thin rag for a bed.

Then one day, while carrying water home from the well, the donkey's leg went lame.

Immediately he tumbled over, spilling the water.

And when he tried to walk again, his leg had gone wonky.

Oh no!

And he was zig-a-zagging this way and that way across the road.

What was worse, when his owner saw the empty buckets, he went boiling mad.

"You're a donkey that's wonky!" he shouted. "You're not worth a bean.

You're the worst working donkey that I've ever seen!"

And he kicked the donkey's bottom once, twice, three times.

So the donkey had to run away lickety split, even though his hoof was hurting.

The donkey zig-a-zag-zigged along the track, wobbling into the verge, and out of it, for miles and miles, until he came to a ramshackle farm where a busy farmer was hurling seeds into the ground.

"Please sir," said the donkey, "have you a job I could do? Just the tiniest job, just for one day or two?"

"Okay," said the farmer, "my potato field needs a big plough. Get hold of a plough and plough that field now."

Well, the donkey did his best.

A thousand times up and a thousand times down he dragged the plough, till his grey fur was completely brown with mud.

But when he had finished the furrows, they weren't straight as they were supposed to be, but twisty and curly.

This sent the farmer hopping mad.

"You're a donkey that's wonky!" he shouted. "You're not worth a bean. You're the worst working donkey that I've ever seen!"

And he kicked the donkey's bottom once, twice, three times.

So again the donkey had to run away lickety split, even though his hoof was really hurting.

The donkey zig-a-zag-zigged along the track, wobbling into the verge, and out of it, for miles and miles.

Until eventually he came to a beach – the first time he had seen one.

And there was a man selling donkey rides for a penny.

"Please sir," said the donkey, "have you a job I could do? Just the tiniest job, just for one day or two?"

"Okay," said the man, "that lady there wants a ride. Get her onto your back and go along the seaside."

Well, the donkey did his best.

He staggered past the beach balls and brollies, but no matter how hard he tried, he couldn't stop wobbling.

In fact, he wobbled right off the beach and into a busy road.

"Help! Help! HELP!" squealed the lady, and the cars started up a terrific tooting and honking.

This sent the donkey-ride man steaming mad.

"You're a donkey that's wonky!" he shouted. "You're not worth a bean. You're the worst working donkey that I've ever seen!"

And he kicked the donkey's bottom once, twice, three times.

So again the donkey had to run away lickety split, even though his hoof was really, really hurting.

The donkey zig-a-zag-zigged along the track, wobbling into the verge, and out of it for miles and miles, until eventually he came to a big house with lots of tall windows and beautiful gardens at the front and back.

A round, red-faced man was standing at the gate.

"Please sir," said the donkey, "have you a job I could do? Just the tiniest job, just for one day or two?"

"Well listen," said the man, "it's funny we met. My girl's lost her cat and she needs a good pet."

And he took the donkey to meet his daughter, Sophie, who jumped with joy when she saw his huge floppy ears and sad eyes.

When he was stronger, the donkey didn't mind giving Sophie rides because she was so light.

In fact he did virtually everything for her: digging holes in her sandpit, even pushing her on the swing with his nose.

She always made sure the straw in his shed was clean and his water fresh.

Sophie grew to love him more than anything in the world.

For the first time in his life the donkey was truly happy.

Until one day the father came running in a panic.

"I don't know what to do!" he cried. "Something's not right! Sophie hasn't come home and it's now nearly night."

Without saying a word, the donkey walked out to look for her.

He zig-a-zag-zigged along the track, wobbling into the verge, and out of it for miles and miles.

Slowly the skies turned grey, then dark, then the rain whipped down onto the donkey's back like a bad memory.

And then over the howl of the wind he heard...

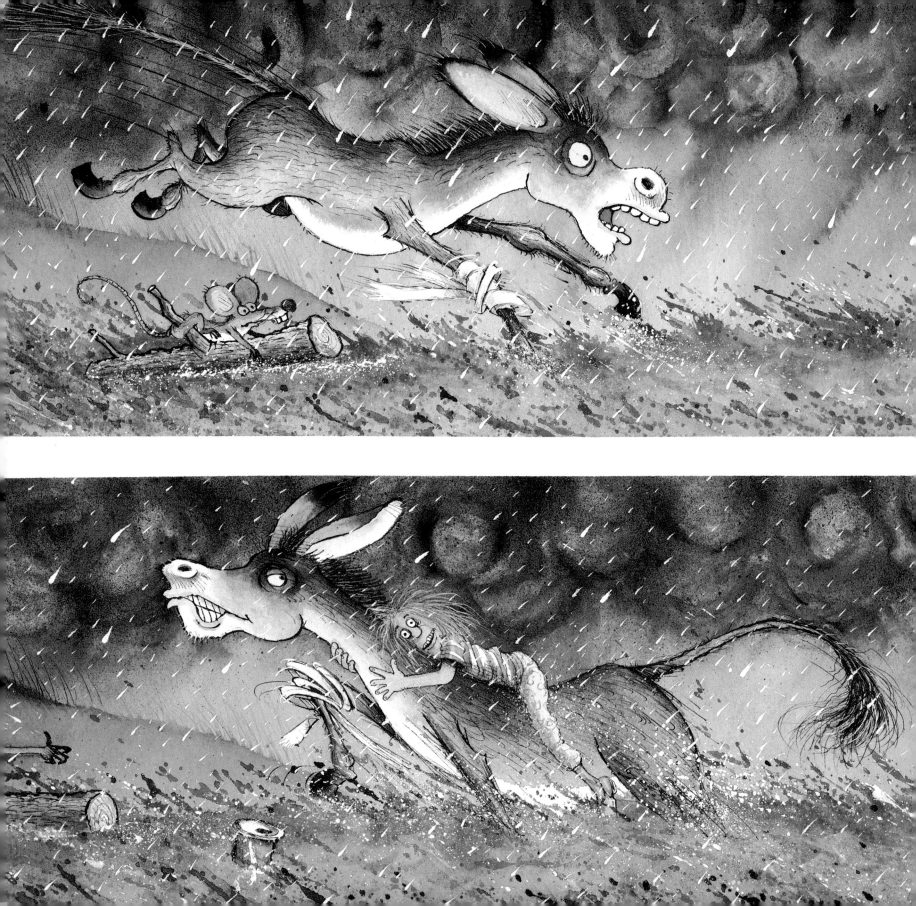

...a smaller cry.

A cry of panic from the little girl who had fallen into the river.

Without a thought for the danger the donkey plunged into the water and set out for the middle, paddling splish-a-splash-splish with his three good legs.

When he reached his beloved Sophie he shouted, "Sophie my girl, now use all of your might, grab hold of my back and hold on tight!"

And he turned for the shore with the rain in his ears and nose, and started paddling, splish-a-splash-splish.

Going slower and slower.

Splish... a... splash... splish.

Until with his last drop of strength he struggled up onto the bank.

"Pthew!" Sophie spat out water from her mouth.

But then, just as quickly, tears filled her eyes. The donkey was lying very still at her feet.

She ran back as fast as she could to her village for help.

But when the people came to help, it was too late.

The donkey's long hard life was over.

Gently Sophie's father and his best friend lifted the donkey's body onto their shoulders and carried him back.

It was the first time people had seen men carrying a donkey, rather than the other way round.

And later they built a brass statue of him
in the village square: brass ears, brass nose,
right down to four brass hooves.
People came from far around to see it.
Children skipped, people took days off work,
and even the farmer and the donkey-ride
owner came to say sorry.

They all stopped and stared, and they
nodded when they read the brass plaque
beneath. It said…

To remember his limp is to remember just part,
For the wonkiest donkey was the firmest of heart.